Art Kills

Other novels by Eric Van Lustbader

Art Kills

Eric Van Lustbader

An Otto Penzler Book

CARROLL & GRAF PUBLISHERS

NEW YORK

ART KILLS

Carroll & Graf Publishers
An Imprint of Avalon Publishing Group Inc.
161 William St., 16th Floor
New York, NY 10038

First Carroll & Graf edition 2002

Library of Congress Cataloging-in-Publication Data is available.

ISBN: 0-7867-0889-1

Printed in the United States of America
Distributed by Publishers Group West

Art Kills

I t was a strange, sultry day in Manhattan. A cadmium yellow sky smudged with clouds and wind-whipped debris arced over Fifth Avenue like an unfinished painting. And, as I say, there was a certain strangeness in the air that made my nostrils flare.

It being lunchtime, I was at my accustomed sidewalk table at Max's, the restaurant occupying the ground floor of the landmark hotel across the avenue from the Empire State Museum of Art. It is a truism that food, no matter how deliciously prepared, lacks a certain piquancy without a view from which to savor it. Traffic whizzed by the beautiful white stone facade of that treasure trove where these days I spend a good deal of my time. My father had taken me to this very museum when I was six, introducing me to Picasso, Monet, and Seurat. Years later, just before he sent me off to school in Paris, we again found ourselves in the high galleries. To his delight, it was I who pointed

1

out the stylistic nuances I had been taught about the artists he so adored. I did this faultlessly not because it was what he wanted, but because by that time I was wearing his passion for art as comfortably as a silk slip.

When he had seen me off at the airport, he had said, "Take in everything, Tess; reject nothing. This is the artist's secret."

I reached into my handbag for my agenda to check my afternoon appointments. I like to think that my father would have been proud of the business I had built up finding and examining paintings for private clients. In any event, since over his lifetime he had given the museum a great deal of money, he would have been pleased that I donate time each week to combing their permanent collection in search of fakes. That was one of my specialties.

It was sad that I would never really know my father's reactions to what I had become; I had just been starting out when the first of his strokes felled him. My father had made his considerable fortune extracting elements both precious and mundane from the earth. Because of this, I feel sure, he harbored a great need to give back something of what he had plundered.

In all ways he had been a closed man—shut

tight as a clam. No one had really known him—not even my mother, *especially* not my mother, who had run off to Europe with an Italian count of dubious repute—save me. In his image, I had perfected a grave and penetrating gaze that gave the impression that I had neither humor nor a lightness of spirit. This suited me perfectly, since I could see no earthly reason for offering my true nature like a lamb to anyone the wind blew in my direction. When I was growing up my father spent hours teaching me how to play poker. He said it was the best way he could think of to teach me about life. He taught me that winning in poker depends on two things: memory and emotion. You had to have a whole lot of one and none of the other. I was such an adept pupil that when I was older, he would occasionally bring me into his high-stakes games as a ringer so we could both clean up.

Willie arrived with my lunch—seared trout over wilted spinach. I inquired about his wife and three children, and he thanked me yet again for helping him find a tutor for his dyslexic eldest son. This tutor was too dear for Willie to afford so I had instructed him to quote a price half his usual fee. I made up the difference without anyone being the wiser. Willie asked me how

3

Peter was and I told him that Peter and I had broken up. That was a shame, Willie said. Peter was such a nice young man.

I sighed. As usual, Willie was right on the mark. Peter was a nice young man. He was also crazy about me. That hadn't stopped me from pushing him away; in fact, it might have been a contributing factor. Peter had been the fourth nice young man I'd dated in the two years since my father's death. In the eighteen months between my father's two strokes I'd been too busy working and tending to him for any kind of social life.

There was a hole inside me into which all these nice young men plunged like stones, sinking without a trace. Take Peter, for instance. He was kind and sweet and generous. He also knew how to kiss. But he hadn't been able to touch me deep down where it mattered, so when he wanted to take our relationship to the next logical level, I told him as gently as I knew how that I could not. I hadn't disliked any of them; I simply hadn't felt anything at all. While it was true that when I saw them more often than not I had fun, the moment they left my side they disappeared from my consciousness as if they had never existed. What was wrong with me?

I looked down at my trout, which by now had

lost all its heat. No matter; I had no appetite for it anyway. Thinking about my shortcomings made me as depressed as when studying a bleak Vlaminck landscape.

I had just ordered a single-malt Scotch when I happened to spot Howard Lenz hurrying down the museum's expansive front stairs, a well-worn leather briefcase clutched in one fist. He was sweating like an ice-monkey at a Hawaiian wedding. If my mind had not wandered into dangerous and unpleasant territory, my curiosity might never have been piqued, but I needed an immediate distraction and Lenz was it. It was just after one-thirty. All the curators were in an interdepartmental conference, and had been so for an hour. What was Lenz, a dodgy little art dealer, doing exiting the museum now? Knowing his rather sordid predilections as I did, it was a sure bet he hadn't been inside admiring the artwork.

Lenz, with a rather awkwardly distracted look on his ferret-like face, stepped off the curb and scurried across Fifth Avenue on his bandy little legs. He was heading more or less directly toward me, though in his agitated state he had not yet seen me. His long, yellow-white hair was slicked down, tied in back in a ponytail that had long since gone out of style. It shone in the sunlight like a helmet. He was almost across when he spotted me. Oddly, a smile broke out on his face and I'm sure he was just about to say something when a large black sedan running the red light on Eightieth Street plowed right into him. Lenz, looking quite stunned, was hurled into the side of a parked white Lexus and dragged all the way to the car's front end, where he fetched up against the rear bumper of the Chrysler parked just in front.

I describe this horrific scene in retrospect. At the time, it was merely a blur. All that registered was Lenz's body bouncing like a ball off the side of the white Lexus, and blood exploding like paint on a Pollock canvas. My stomach seemed to rise up into my throat, threatening to disgorge its contents.

People were screaming, running from every direction. An elderly woman at a table next to mine fainted, adding to the confusion and panic. Crowds formed as if from thin air, teeming like ants over a mound of earth. I joined them, slipping over the restaurant's low, wrought-iron railing. I could see Lenz's face now, horribly smeared with blood. Some teeth were outside his lower lip, as if he had been struck down like a mad dog. There was no question of him being alive, I could see that. When one has lived in Europe as I have, one comes to recognize death, which has a different significance than it does in America. In Paris and Venice, I had lived in apartments and villas where people had died, sometimes generations of them. The stonework, the small exquisite gardens, the interior beams are all infused with the blood of the dead, a patina that becomes one's connection to history.

"For God's sake, call the police!" I shouted to Dominic, the maitre d', who nodded as if waking from a trance, and hurried into the restaurant.

The crowd, weaned on electronic voyeurism, pressed in, hungry for their view of the carnage. Through the mounting frenzy, I saw a pencil-thin man with a long El Greco face expertly making his way toward the inner edge of people. He never pushed or shoved people aside, but rather took advantage of the tiny pockets of space that developed within the jostling throng. At the edge of the curb, he flexed his knees and scooped up the briefcase Lenz had been clutching. Producing a handkerchief, he quickly wiped off the blood. In one fluid motion he was up and moving away. He walked neither quickly nor slowly, but in an altogether normal manner so as not to draw attention to himself.

Instinctively, I followed him. I was both outraged and intrigued. I remember thinking that if Lenz couldn't do anything about this theft, I would. Not that I had any love for Lenz. As I said, he was a filthy little creature who made his dubious living off of people too ignorant to know that what he was purveying was often as phony as his Austrian accent. The weasel had been born in Canarsie; he'd never even set foot in Vienna, let alone been born and raised there as he claimed. And yet, looting the dead seemed to me so indecent, so despicable that I could not simply turn my back on it. I could hear my father, protector of the underdog, urging me on. Justice would be done Lenz, even though in life he'd had no concept of the word himself.

Besides, I had a desire to find out just what it was Lenz had in the briefcase.

The man with the El Greco face ducked into a late-model Ford parked on Seventy-eighth Street. As he turned over the ignition I hailed a cab. We went through the Seventy-ninth Street Transverse, with me following the Ford while giving elaborate hand signals to the cabbie. I'd tried English and French, but apparently he spoke only Farsi.

We emerged from the park, heading west until

the Ford ran the light on West End Avenue, leaving us stalled in traffic. I threw some bills through the scarred plastic divider, leapt out of the taxi and, dodging cars, ran down the street. The Ford headed up West End, and then made a hard left onto Eighty-third. I sprinted up the block, made the light, and crossed the avenue in time to see the man with the El Greco face double-park his car in front of an old pre-war apartment building. When he got out I could see he held Lenz's battered briefcase under one arm. He was holding it as if it was filled with eggs.

By that time, I was halfway down the block. I went into the building so close after him he held the door open for me. I said something under my breath, then rummaged in my handbag as if looking for my key. He opened the lock on the inner door and, with another murmur of thanks, I stepped through after him. The lobby smelled of old lives, as if each separate scent was a sepia-toned snapshot of its long-ago inhabitants. There was no one in it but us.

I ducked into the mailbox alcove, turned right around, and peeked out. The man with the El Greco face stepped into the elevator, the door closed, and I sprinted across the lobby. I pressed the elevator call button as I saw the indicator stop at the seventh floor. When the elevator returned to the lobby, I took it up.

Arriving on the seventh floor, I was faced with another dilemma. Which apartment had my quarry gone into? There were five on the floor, which told me they had been spared the brutal downsizing some people called modernization. As I made my slow, careful circuit of the hallway, I noticed that one door appeared unlatched. Sure enough, when I turned the knob and pushed ever so gently, I found myself inside the apartment. It had one of those long entryways that led into the living room. Black-and-white photos of a sleek-hulled ketch lined both walls. In one of them, I could make out the three faces of the crew standing just aft of the mizzenmast: two men and a woman. One man was older, the other two a generation younger. The older man looked familiar. I was racking my brains to put a name to his face when I heard a noise like the skittling of a baby's rattle bouncing across the floor.

I went quickly down the hall and peered around the corner. The living room—all browns and taupes and beiges, in a classic 1930s color scheme—looked comfortable and empty. Through the west-facing windows the leafy trees of Riverside Park provided a frame for a lovely composition of the Hudson River and the New Jersey palisades Frederick Church would have greatly admired. As I peeked out a little farther, I could see the open archway into a cozy-looking kitchen the color of butterscotch. Further to my right, a short hallway led straight down a hall to a bedroom. I froze. Through the open doorway I could see two men struggling. One of them was the man with the El Greco face.

What the hell was going on?

I crossed the Oriental rug, took my high-heels off, and went down the inner hallway. The thin, bloodless lips of the man with the El Greco face were drawn back, revealing a set of tobacco-stained teeth that reminded me of my father's antique ivory chess set. Breath hissed out between his clenched teeth, in that odd, skittling sound, sending a small chill down my spine.

I was also close enough to see that the other man was big and beefy in the manner of a professional wrestler or bodyguard. His bunched-up muscles put so many wrinkles in his suit jacket you would have thought it was made of crepe paper. Both men were concentrating so hard that I could have lifted my skirt and neither would have noticed.

The bull was in the process of strangling the

man with the El Greco face. Not that I cared. On the contrary, I could feel the outrage that had brought me to this moment silently egging him on. Now that he was taking care of the man with the El Greco face, I turned my attention to finding Lenz's briefcase. I had come this far; I wasn't going to leave without it.

I saw it on the bedspread and leaned over toward it. Unfortunately, the man with the El Greco face chose that moment to expire, and the bull, no doubt seeing movement out of the corner of his eye, glanced up.

"Fuck!" he said, and reached for a gun I saw lying on the floor where I assumed the man with the El Greco face had kicked it. He was probably expecting me to go white in the face and yell "Eek!" Instead, I lunged toward him and as the gun swung toward me, slammed him on the top of the head with the heel of my shoe. He toppled over, making an odd mewling sound. As I reached over him, snatching up the briefcase, he grabbed the hem of my skirt. I could see from his expression that he was semi-conscious, so I drove my knee into the side of his head. I felt the contact all the way into my hip.

I had to pry his fingers off the material, then I was out of there. In the hallway, I put on my shoes.

Then, not wanting to run into anyone, I took the fire stairs all the way down to the lobby. Once or twice my knee, unhappy about the abuse I had subjected it to, nearly gave way. On the third floor landing I stretched it out so that by the time I reached the lobby it felt fine. I stayed inside the stairwell while an elderly couple shuffled through the lobby. They took so long I wanted to scream. I had no idea how long the bull would be unconscious, but I had no intention of being anywhere in the vicinity when he regained consciousness.

At last, the couple reached the elevator and, striding across the lobby, I made my hasty exit. Out on the street, the sunlight seemed blinding, colors supersaturated. My heart was beating hard and fast in my chest and, to my horror, my hands were trembling. I hurried to West End Avenue and hailed a cab.

All the way downtown I watched in a daze the city blur by me as the taxi sped through midtown, Chelsea, the Village, then into Soho. I was dying to know what was inside the briefcase, but after everything that had happened since I had first seen it, I felt an odd kind of superstition that compelled me to keep it closed until I was safely inside my apartment. I say "odd" because I am not by nature a superstitious person. I don't give a fig about

Friday the thirteenth or care if I step under a ladder or on a crack in the sidewalk. But in this case two people were dead and another had been injured. Already a certain aura had commenced to encircle this battered briefcase. I found that I was clutching it to my breast, much as Lenz had done as he had hurried down the Empire's grand stone staircase.

With a sigh of relief, I turned the keys in the upper and lower Medeco locks and entered my loft apartment. The high-pitched beeping of the security system ceased when I punched the code into the wall-mounted keypad.

Then, as I always did, I lighted the dozen candles I had scattered about the main living space, and gazed at my old friends hanging on the walls—paintings by Picasso, Monet, Dufy, Cézanne, Degas, Manet, Delacroix, and Renoir. Many of them I had inherited from my father, but others I had acquired on my own. They were like my children, these pieces of history, these blissful doorways into the true glory of the world, the pinnacle of man's achievements. With only the soft, diffused illumination drifting through the room these paintings had the appearance of an intimate gathering of dinner guests who, having long ago shed their mortal coils, had nevertheless left behind a distinct aura of intent.

After a time, I hit the light switch and turned on the stereo. Miles Davis's exotic *Sketches of Spain* flooded the room. I poured myself a very large Oban Scotch, and took a deep sip as I watched the last of the afternoon's sunlight burnish the scuffed and scarred leather briefcase. The thing seemed to breathe like a winded animal.

I sat down and without a moment's further hesitation opened it up. I pulled out a soft, square package, swaddled in a protected skin of bubble wrap. As I peeled off the layers of plastic I could see an image emerging.

It was a small painting, unframed and unlovely. No Old Master or Postimpressionist had created this. It was a rather stiff and awkward portrait of a woman of indefinite age. There was no life whatsoever in her face. I picked it up and held it in front of me. I wondered what poor sucker Lenz had targeted to buy this worthless painting—one could hardly call it art. Well, I had done my good deed for the day, that was certain. On the other hand, what was Lenz doing with this at the museum? And, even more puzzling, why was this homely painting the object of so much violence?

I continued to study the portrait. As far as I could see, there was nothing in the least out of the ordinary about it. It was the kind of thing one might see anywhere around the city for a couple of hundred dollars. Sipping on my Scotch, I brought it into my studio where I routinely checked paintings for authenticity. I scraped off a piece of pigment from the lower left-hand corner and checked its date. An hour later—after completing my series of chemical tests—I had determined by the level of lead that, indeed, the painting had been done in the 1940s. Nothing extraordinary about that, surely. Then why had the man with the El Greco face gone to the trouble of snatching it from Lenz? And why had he, in turn, been murdered by the bull? It made no sense.

I put the painting aside, and picked up the phone. I stared at it as I ordered hot and sour soup, an egg roll, and Kung Pao Chicken, extra hot, from my local Chinese take-out. It was getting late, and I hadn't eaten much of Max's trout. As I cradled the receiver I noticed something. The angle of light changed and I chanced to see a darker area in the corner where I had scraped off the pigment. I peered at it through my overhead lighted magnifier, and sure enough, there was paint underneath. That was typical. Almost all painters coated bare canvas with pigment so their colors would take better. This, however, appeared different. The hue was a deep umber, making it extremely unlikely that any artist would have used it to "cure" his canvas.

Using a combination of chemicals, I carefully stripped off a larger section of the portrait. Now, through the lens of my magnifier, I could see that the texture of the pigment was altogether different from that of the painting on top. I recognized that texture and tone, and my heart skipped a beat.

Miles Davis's music faded, the walls fell away from the studio and I was alone, floating in the infinite of history with this square of canvas, wood, and pigment. I felt a mounting frenzy grip me and I tried to calm myself. But as I worked I could hear the beating of the painting's long-buried heart.

When I was halfway done I knew that I was looking at a genuine Raphael. The color palette of rich, muted umbers that abruptly faded to pale gold and pinks as light from an unseen source struck the subject, the beautifully controlled brushwork made the work unmistakable. What I couldn't figure out was the subject itself. It looked like none of the great master's paintings, and believe me I am familiar with the entire œuvre.

It wasn't until I had washed away the last of the execrable portrait that I knew what I held in my hands. This was a portrait, delicate, breathtaking, erotically intimate, of Venus rising from the sea. Ever since my first trip to Venice I had heard stories, unsubstantiated rumors that Raphael had painted his own rendition of the birth of the Greek goddess that Botticelli had made famous. That was unsurprising, since Raphael's powerful fresco of the nymph Galatea was inspired by the same poem by the Florentine Angelo Poliziano that had fired Botticelli's brush. Though the Raphael Venus was described in a number of texts, no one in the current art world had claimed to have seen it—in fact, some scholars argued it never existed. And so it had slipped into the realm of legend.

But I had seen this painting once before—or, rather, a painting Lenz had claimed to be Raphael's Venus. By exposing it as a fake, albeit an exceedingly clever one, I had cost Lenz an enormous commission. At first, he'd seemed bitter about that, and had at every opportunity tried to smear my reputation. When that had failed, he had lapsed into a kind of stylized chumminess that would have been inappropriate if it hadn't had about it the heavy stench of irony.

Speaking of ironic, now somehow Lenz had come into possession of the real Raphael Venus. The legend had come to life, the portrait was just as it had been described in the now not-so-apocryphal texts. This painting was virtually priceless.

No wonder two men were dead. I had been suspicious of Lenz's death from the first. Now it was easy for me to understand the lengths someone would go to procure such a rare and magnificent painting. This was art on the most exalted level.

Venus, immersed in early morning sunlight, gazed out at me from her dark eyes at once enigmatic and laughing. What had she been thinking at the moment of her birth? Using the alchemy of genius, Raphael had infused the goddess with a serenity as vibrant as it was numinous. In this altogether astonishing portrait, he had made certain that one could recognize in the goddess's face all the stages of life—childhood, adolescence, adulthood, old age.

I was rapt by the magic Raphael had wrought. I could not take my eyes off his vision of Venus, even when the downstairs buzzer rang. Reluctant to leave my new friend, I put her away. Then I went back through the apartment to the intercom. My take-out order had arrived and I buzzed in the delivery boy. I was fumbling through my purse when the doorbell rang.

"Just a minute," I called as I fished my wallet out and unlocked the door. Two men shouldered their way in. Neither of them was Chinese.

"Hello, Ms. Chase," the one with the silver hair said.

"Do I know you?"

"Not really," he said with a smile that meant nothing. "But I know you."

"Is that meant to be a joke?"

"Carmine don't make jokes," the other man said. He had hair the color and texture of a stoat's pelt, and there was so much green in his complexion that he looked half-dead.

"That's Leon," Carmine said. "Don't mind him; he's got no sense of humor."

"Carmine, Leon—fine, we've been introduced," I said. They both wore sharkskin suits, and ties that were meant to be fashionable but were simply loud. "Now what are you doing in my apartment?"

"Delivering the chinks," Carmine said, handing me a large, warm brown bag. I could smell the stir-fried chilies and fresh cilantro.

"Really. You two don't look like delivery boys."

"Depends on what's bein' delivered," Leon grinned as he grabbed his crotch.

"Shut up," Carmine snapped.

I put the bag down on the sideboard. "Okay, gentlemen, your fun is over. I'm going to ask you to leave."

Leon guffawed and Carmine glared at him.

"We got a little business with you, Ms. Chase," Carmine said with that same millimeter-thin smile. It was really quite a ghastly thing.

"I don't think so," I said, heading for the front door to usher them out.

As I came abreast of him, Leon grabbed my elbow. At the same time, he slipped a Glock .38 automatic from beneath his armpit and laid the barrel between my breasts.

"Fer Christ's sake, would you cut that out," Carmine said. "This is a lady. Put the cannon away."

Leon grunted, clearly annoyed. But he did as he was told.

"My God, do you ever brush your teeth?" I said to him. Carmine chuckled as I shook myself loose and turned to him. "Would you mind telling me what this is all about?"

"No problem," he said. "We came for the painting."

"What painting?"

"See, Carmine," Leon said, circling me, "I fuckin' told you."

Carmine, ignoring his compatriot, had a pained look on his face. "We've only just met, Ms. Chase. Let's not get off on the wrong foot."

"I think it's too late for that."

"I'm afraid in my line of work I don't have time to study Miss Manners."

"And that line of work would be . . .?"

He made a curling gesture with his fingers. "Just give up the painting you stole."

"Tell me something, Carmine." I crossed my arms over my chest. "Is it possible to steal something that's already stolen?"

"I so much wanna hit this skirt upside her head," Leon growled, still circling.

"Y'know, Ms. Chase, much as I hate to agree with him, Leon has a point."

"Only on the top of his head."

That was when Leon grabbed me. He put his stinking mouth on mine and, taking two handfuls of my buttocks, jammed my groin against his. I looked him calmly in the eye and lifted my knee hard into his genitals. He gave a little grunt and, doubling over, let me go. I stepped away from him.

"I admire your fearlessness, Ms. Chase, really I

do." Carmine's face was growing dark. "But you'd be smart to get the painting."

"Just keep the beast away from me," I said. I didn't want him to think I was a fool so I got the painting and laid it in the bubble-wrap. I got a roll of tape out of the third drawer of the metal tabouret next to my work desk. Carmine lounged against the open doorway as I slid the painting into Lenz's battered briefcase. "Okay. Now what?" I put the roll of tape back into the open drawer, right next to the .32 Beretta Tomcat semi-automatic I had recently bought to replace the .25 my father had given me on my sixteenth birthday. The Tomcat, though less than fifteen inches long, had the stopping power of a powerful .380. My father had taught me how to use pistols, as well as how to defend myself in as many other ways as he could think of. There were a whole lot more than I could have at that age imagined.

"Ms. Chase, I strongly urge you to close that drawer," Carmine said, coming up beside me. "I know you don't wanna give up that painting, but believe me when I tell you I don't want you t'get hurt."

The odd thing was I did believe him. I nodded and shut the drawer. "Take the damn painting," I said.

"No, you take it," he said as he turned on his heel. Then he gave me that millimeter-thin smile. "Maybe that painting's worth a fortune; maybe it isn't worth crap. Either way, you're gonna tell the boss which."

We drove out to the eastern end of Long Island. I sat in the front seat next to Carmine. Leon sat directly behind me, the muzzle of his Glock just touching the nape of my neck. I could smell his sour breath all the way.

"I hurt," he said to me once as he ground the muzzle into my neck.

"Leon, cut it the fuck out," Carmine told him, and the beast was still.

We turned off Route 27 in Wainscott, and Carmine drove slowly through the estate section that fronted Georgica Pond. I had been out here several times during the summer months, having been invited by clients. I knew how many millions it took to buy a house in this area, and how many thousands it took to maintain it each year.

We stopped in front of a pair of electronically controlled gates. Carmine punched in a code on

the box that stood there, the gates swung sound-
lessly open, and we turned into a long curving
driveway of white crushed shells. On either side,
perfect rows of cherry trees marched up toward a
huge, two-story clapboard house with a multitude
of gables and deep eaves. We passed emerald
lawns as flat and tidy as a golf course fairway.

Leon seemed to disappear the moment we got
inside the house. Carmine took me through the
oval entryway from which a magnificent teak
stairway curved up to the second floor. The living
room was expansive and light. Sets of French
doors looked out onto more lawn that dropped
down to the pond, a rather large body of water
that went all the way south to the barrier beach
and the Atlantic Ocean.

Carmine led me into the library. Even though
I'd seen only a small portion of the house, I'd
passed two paintings by Matisse, a small Rodin,
three works by Degas, and a set of Picasso draw-
ings. Nothing daring or avant-garde. That jibed
with the color scheme, which began in the
entryway with ecru and vanilla, progressed to sand
and now, in the library, deepened to mahogany and
siena. I took a quick inventory of the works of art.
Some of them I was intimately familiar with,
having attended the auctions at Sotheby's and

Christie's where they had, variously, appeared for sale. All had been bought over the phone by an anonymous bidder.

Bach's Toccata and Fugue in D Minor was playing from hidden speakers. Two people broke off a conversation when they saw us. The man was tall and distinguished looking, handsome in a vaguely predatory way, with wings of silver hair at his temples. He wore cream-colored wool trousers, a crisp white shirt with maroon stripes, and oxblood loafers without socks. In short, he was a man comfortable with himself and with the pressures of power. The woman had short blond hair, green eyes, and a generous mouth. She was a petite thing, dressed in black: trim slacks and a clingy leotard top. She wore lipstick, but no other makeup. She had no need of it; she was astonishingly—almost magnetically—attractive. Her eyes followed me with a kind of intense curiosity wherever I went in the room.

"This is Tess Chase," Carmine said as if introducing me to the room at large. Then he disappeared.

"My name is Richard Sanborne." I could not have said precisely why, but when this man spoke everything in the room changed. The furniture became darker and more deeply placed within their setting, and the ceiling pressed down as if overladen with its rococo plaster scrollwork. From the first, I was aware of a certain lack in him. Despite his confidence, his polish, there was a yawning emptiness at the core of him, as if at some dark time in the past his soul had been excised. Even the hardiest spirit could easily tremble before someone like that.

Sanborne ignored the woman standing behind him, but I couldn't. She looked familiar and, in a flash, I had it. I had seen her in the photo at the apartment where the man with the El Greco face had been murdered. She had been standing beside an older man, a man whose name now echoed ominously inside my head: Rocco Bravanno, the last of the great East Coast crime bosses. This must be Rocco's daughter; he had been a handsome man and in person I could see the resemblance.

"Your reputation in the art world precedes you, Ms. Chase," Sanborne was saying. "I consider it my great good fortune to meet you." He smiled as he took the briefcase out of my hand. The way he slit open the bubble-wrap made me wince inside.

"What is this?" he said as he took it into the light. "What have you uncovered?"

"Is it a Raphael?" the woman said with quickened breath. I must say I was startled that she would recognize the great master's style from an unknown example of his work. I returned my attention to her. She possessed a sensual intensity that was so close to the surface it seemed positively febrile. This was a quality I had never before encountered and it so intrigued me that for some moments I was totally absorbed by her when I should have been concentrating on Sanborne, who was the immediate threat.

To his question I at first said nothing. I wanted very much to lie, to tell him the masterpiece was nothing more than an imitation, but that would be foolish. Sanborne would only find another expert with less scruples who would tell him the truth. Then, doubtless, he would dispatch Carmine or Leon to come after me. I felt like Odysseus between Scylla and Charybdis: if I lied the monster would kill me, but if I told the truth the great whirlpool would suck away the thing I wanted most: the Raphael. "It is, indeed, a genuine Raphael," I said at length.

Sanborne turned to me. "Really? How gratifying." He turned to the woman and in a clipped tone ordered her to get me a drink. "You've no doubt had a difficult day," he said to me.

"Unusual, yes," I said. "Difficult, no." To the woman, I said, "Do you have Oban? It's—"

"A single-malt Scotch. I know." She went to the portable bar, opened a decanter, poured, and handed me the glass. No one else was drinking but what the hell; Sanborne was right: it *had* been a difficult day. As I sipped my drink, I observed him. My father taught me that the better you know the man you're up against the more ways you'll find to defeat him. After his initial look, which was little more than cursory, Sanborne appeared to have precious little interest in the Raphael. He was a philistine, I decided. Simply because someone surrounded himself with art didn't mean he knew how to appreciate it. Sanborne was a trophy-jockey. One look at the woman was enough to convince me of that.

"Do you know what the Raphael is worth?" I asked him.

"I know its potential on a certain very private market. That's what it's worth."

"No, Mr. Sanborne. Its worth has already been measured by the death of two people, not to mention the abduction at gunpoint of another, namely me. Whatever your prospective buyer is willing to pay is irrelevant. This Raphael belongs in a museum."

"Well, there's a novel opinion for you." He seemed lost in thought for a moment. "Ms. Chase, would you excuse me? Jacqueline will see to whatever you need."

"I need to get out of here," I said, putting down my glass.

Either he didn't hear me or he chose not to. The music finished. Rocco Bravanno's daughter and I regarded each other in the sudden silence of the room. I said, "Must I stay cooped up?"

"Not at all." She had a nice smile. It was easy and unforced, totally unlike the hard, artificial smiles of the men around here. "Would you like to go outside?"

"Very much."

She led me back into the living room where I saw Carmine lurking, a clear reminder, no doubt, that I was not free to leave. She ushered me through a set of French doors, out onto a vast flagstone patio that surrounded a free-form pool and attached Jacuzzi. Expensive lawn furniture was scattered about. At one edge of the patio I could see a putting green and a steeply banked sand trap.

It was getting on toward evening. While I'd been in the library, the sun had slipped below the horizon, but the last of its burnt-orange fire informed the sky with the exact color of the dress in which Raphael had dressed his Maddelena.

"How did you recognize the Raphael?" I asked her.

"I spent my senior year in college in Venice, studying art and politics," she said. "It was my father's idea. I liked it so much I stayed on until Richard came and married me."

She took off her suede slipper-shoes and left them on the edge of the patio as she stepped off into the damp grass. I did the same as I followed her down the sloping lawn toward the water. Far out, across the pond, in among thick stands of trees, I could see the dark silhouettes of other mansions. To their right was the charcoal smudge of the barrier beach.

"Is Sanborne coming back?" I asked.

"Oh, yes. Eventually."

"Pity."

"Yes. A great pity."

She was able to impart so much to me in those few words that I was absolutely certain I knew the nature of her particular fever. To my utter astonishment, I found myself saying: "If you don't love him, you should leave him."

She turned to me, and in her breathless, intense manner, said: "You were thinking of lying to him about the authenticity of the Raphael. Don't bother denying it; I could tell." Her eyes searched mine. "I think about leaving him—every day, every moment. But I don't, for the same reason, I think, you decided to tell him the truth. It was in your best interest."

"But surely staying with him cannot be in *your* best interest." When only silence was forthcoming, I continued: "Does he mistreat you?"

She looked at me candidly. "If by that you mean does he beat me physically, no, never. However 'mistreat' has broader meanings, and pain is felt in so many ways." Her gaze swung away from me toward the far end of the pond where it was pale and flat and formless. "My father used to tell me that physical pain—he was talking then of being shot—is a brief thing, and in time is blessedly forgotten. But I have found that for other pain more subtle, more profound, this is regrettably not so."

Her words brought a shiver as we walked for a time in silence. I felt the cool grass between my toes but derived no great pleasure from it. At last, she said: "Will you tell me about the Raphael?"

I was grateful for the change in subject. "To see it is extraordinary, a once in a lifetime event. To have discovered it. . . ." I let my voice trail off.

"To some it would be akin to finding the Holy Grail."

"And you'd be one of those, wouldn't you, Tess?"

I nodded. "Very much so."

That returned the lovely smile to her lips. "It seems to me you're like a Knight Templar."

"Do I seem so heroic and pure of spirit?" To cover my slight embarrassment, I laughed. "The Knight Templars protected pilgrims during the Second Crusade in the Holy Land. I think we're very far from anyone's definition of the Holy Land."

She came so close to me I could smell the scent of lavender she used, and her expression was anything but light. "You know what I mean. Please don't pretend that you don't," she said softly, her lips moist and half open. "You have an old-fashioned sense of justice, just like my father."

I had difficulty breathing, and found myself absurdly grateful we had arrived at the far edge of the property. Giddy with sudden desire, I leaned against the bole of a tree and tried not to sway. I saw the ketch from the photo tied up to the dock. Its lean, graceful lines were unmistakable.

"That's Rocco Bravanno's ketch," I said.

"It was," Jacqueline acknowledged, "until he was executed by the Russian mafia. They cut off his thumbs; it's their signature." She said this with a soft wail of despair.

I followed her along the water's edge. We were very near the dock where the ketch rocked a little at its mooring. I got the sudden bright idea to sail it across the pond so that I could escape on foot along the barrier beach, but then I saw a figure detach himself from the shadows on the deck. Another guard.

"If my father was still alive I know he'd protect me." Her voice had dropped to a whisper. "I know he'd find a way out of this for me."

I thought about my own strong, vibrant father and how his stroke had left him a disfigured shell of his former self. Living with him I had felt protected from all the evils of the world. And even though he had spent a good part of his life training me to deal with those evils on my own, it was very hard to say goodbye to him. I watched Jacqueline carefully. She had had a strong-willed father, too but, unlike mine, he hadn't adequately prepared her for life after his death. He had, instead, made a calculated mistake in leaving her in the hands of another powerful man. Now, fully in the grip of that power, she needed protecting more than ever. She thought of me as her Knight Templar, and I was astonished to discover that this was precisely what I wanted to be.

"I want you to tell me something," I said. "Did you hire Lenz?"

"Yes, the painting's mine. But my brother Antony found out. He had Lenz killed, making it look like a hit-and-run. His man took the painting to my father's old apartment on West Seventy-third Street, where he used to keep his women, but Richard had his own man waiting for him."

"The big bull."

She smiled. "Sammy needed seventeen stitches to close the wounds you gave him."

"Thank God he's all right." I paused for a moment. "What I don't understand is why you and your brother are on opposite sides."

"Don't you read the tabs?"

"The what?"

"The tabloids." She shook her head. "Of course you don't. After my father's death, the family split into two camps. One was loyal to Richard and to me. The other followed Antony." She shrugged. "Antony's got charisma, and he's a persuasive talker. Anyway, the tabs were way off base, as usual. According to them he and I split because of Richard—my husband's not Italian, not *famiglia*." She shook her head. "But the truth is I caught Antony skimming from the family business. He's got a very expensive habit."

"Gambling?"

She moved us a little farther from the boat where the guard stood watch. "Worse; drugs. He's a stone-cold coke freak." She stuck one pale foot in the water and wriggled her toes, sending ripples outward in a small circle. When she pointed her foot like that she looked like a ballerina. "He desperately wants to run my father's empire on his own, but I don't think he can handle the responsibility. Instead, he's become very dangerous to everyone around him, including me." She shivered. "Richard is the only one who, for the moment at least, can keep Antony in check. Even so, Antony has threatened me several times, and Richard is clever and enough of a bastard to use that to keep me close to him." Her eyes were luminous in the gathering darkness. "Now you see how it is. I can't go forward and I can't go back. I'm like a fly in amber."

A small silence descended. I saw a heron swooping low over the inky water, then wheel away into the gathering darkness.

"Why did you hire a man of questionable reputation like Lenz in the first place?" I asked.

"Richard chose him *because* of his sleazy reputation. He figured that whatever Lenz found out the last thing he'd do was report it to the police or the Feds. With his rep they'd never believe anything he told them."

At the edge of the patio, I saw Sanborne searching for us. He was moving with that certain tension men have when they have something definite on their mind. When she spotted him, an eerie stiffness suffused Jacqueline's body—like the instinctive defense of an animal reacting to its enemy.

She turned to me, pulling me into deep shadow. A weeping willow presented us with a kind of bower that in the suddenly shifting circumstances possessed all the charged exoticism of a Gauguin painting. The long tendrils shivered in the evening breeze, the dusty-green leaves caressed us with a kind of maternal tenderness.

"Tess, you *will* protect me, won't you?" As she embraced me, she gently touched the nape of my neck and I felt a tiny electric thrill shoot down my spine. Something attenuated and ephemeral was being drawn out of my very core. With her fingertips making tiny circles there, she whispered ever so softly: "It's as if my whole life I've been waiting for you."

Then, hearing a sound, she started, and

stepped nimbly out of the bower. I followed her uncertainly just in time to see Sanborne striding down the lawn toward us.

"Sorry I took so long," he said with the air of a man embarking on a disagreeable but necessary chore. "How are you girls getting on?"

Jacqueline spoke without hesitation: "Just showing off our little pond."

"Yeah," Sanborne chuckled, "some little pond." He lighted a cigar and spread his smoke around in the manner of a dog marking out its territory. "So what do you think of the place?"

"It's lovely," I said with some difficulty. Being addressed by Sanborne was like rubbing shoulders with an overseer: one never knew whether to speak up or to flinch at the crack of his whip.

"'Lovely,' she says," he laughed unpleasantly as he blew out smoke. "This is a fucking power spot, honey, that's what it is." And he rattled off the names of the super-rich and famous who were his neighbors. I could see Jacqueline's eyes glittering venomously in the darkness. "The old man, rest his soul, really knew how to live." He tapped the side of his head. "And smart, but he got in over his head with those fucking Russian bastards. They've got no soul; they took advantage of his good will."

He reached into an inside pocket and drew out a thick manila envelope, which he handed over to me. "Five thousand dollars. For services rendered. That's your normal fee, I believe."

"Yes, it is." I put the envelope back into his hand. "But I don't want your money."

"Why not? You did your job."

"I don't work for you," I said. "I never would."

"Ms. Chase, please." Jacqueline pressed the envelope into my hand and closed my fingers around it. I saw something in her eyes, a kind of fever like a fuse burning dangerously close to the end, and I became momentarily frightened that he might, despite her protestations, strike her.

"You earned this money," Sanborne said as if looking down on me from a great height. "Don't insult me by refusing it." Instantaneously, the air was thick with menace.

I smiled pleasantly at him as I took the money. I disliked intensely being in his power, and could almost feel Jacqueline's anguish. There was something smoothly impregnable about him that made you certain you would want for nothing in your platinum prison save your freedom, that he would appreciate you in his own way, like a fine Corot, at all times showing you off to your best advantage. Though I detested him, for her sake I did not want to insult him. Without looking at her, I put the envelope in my handbag.

Sanborne invited me to stay for a late dinner, but I refused. That seemed to come as no great surprise to him, principally because he had put nothing of himself into the pro forma invitation. Since he had other pressing business to attend to it was left to Jacqueline to walk me out to the car that was waiting to take me back to Manhattan. It had begun to drizzle, the ground shimmering with it.

The rear door to the Lincoln Town Car was open and Carmine sat still as a statue behind the wheel. There was another man standing midway between the car and the house. He had this ability to observe us while not looking in our direction. I felt the hairs at the back of my neck stir when I thought of Jacqueline living in her platinum cage.

She walked beside me, deliberately matching her pace with mine. I was so aware of her beside me I had difficulty drawing a breath.

How I could possibly help her was at that moment beyond me. I could see the driveway lights reflected in her eyes as I climbed into the car. I could still feel the furnace of her body, the silken touch of her fingertips that had elicited from me an intimate tremor of response. She stood there, her hair wet with rain as we began to roll smoothly over the driveway. I felt the distance between us, and there was a kind of pain to it, an exquisite pain, as of a fervent wish to prolong a perfect moment. Then Carmine pressed a chrome button, locking all the doors.

It was after midnight when I entered the loft. I turned on every light in the place and spent a surreal ten minutes checking behind doors, under the bed, and in every closet while my heart thudded heavily in my chest. I made sure all the windows were locked. I wondered whether I should get into the habit of pasting one of my hairs across the edge of the front door each time I left. My father had had to do that in Brussels, during the six weeks it took to acquire a company his enemies were interested in buying.

I saw I had a slew of messages on my answering machine, but by this time I was far too exhausted to deal with them. Instead, I lay down on the bed still fully clothed and promptly fell into a deep sleep. I awoke in the middle of the night, my body sexually charged, fully aroused. With difficulty, I fell back to sleep. Toward morning, I dreamed of a beautiful dog in a wire-mesh cage, gnawing itself into bloody ribbons in its desperation to be free.

How nice and reassuring it was, the next morning, to hear the usual litany of phone messages: client queries, art gallery referrals, and museum curator callbacks. My breakfast consisted of a few spoonfuls of cold and gelatinous Kung Pao Chicken, washed down with a cup of steaming Earl Grey tea. The chilies warmed me even more than the tea did. All the way to the Empire State Museum, I thought of Jacqueline in that platinum cage of hers out on the Island. At moments, I felt so close to her I fancied I could feel the cool imprint the bars made on her flesh. I dropped off the envelope with Sanborne's money with my friend Bob Hodges, the director of development, and told him to list it as an anonymous donation. I had known Bob and his wife, Nina, for ten years, having been introduced to them by my father. Over that period the three of us had become close friends. It was to Bob and Nina that I went after all my affairs ended badly. We chatted for a couple of minutes, promised each other we would get together soon for dinner, then I left without remembering a word either of us said.

Outside, gusts of wind were painting the sidewalk with the fountain's spume. Across Fifth Avenue, there was no sign of yesterday's death, not even those yellow crime scene tapes. I hailed a taxi, but one of those large, vaguely sinister-looking black Lincoln Navigators cut the cab off, pulling to a stop right in front of me. The rear door popped open and a man got out. He was almost as large as the Navigator.

"Good morning, Ms. Chase," came a rich baritone from the interior. "I wonder if I may have a word with you."

Peering in, I saw a rakishly handsome man with a rough-hewn face Picasso might have drawn, sun-bleached eyes and thick, curly black hair. I had seen him before, standing on the ketch with Jacqueline and their father.

"And you would be Antony Bravanno. Now I've met the entire family."

"Not yet," he said. "But I aim to rectify that oversight."

When I glanced at the Goliath standing beside me, I could hear Antony chuckle. "Louie's harmless until he's given orders to attack." He chuckled again as if he was his own best audience. "Will you do me the courtesy." I didn't see that I had a choice. He beckoned me in and, ignoring Louie's helping hand, I climbed into the Navigator.

The interior was cavernous, which suited me: I could put plenty of room between me and Antony.

Louie had gone to sit up front with the driver half a football field away.

As we drove off, Antony said to me: "Since you're huddled as far away from me as you can get, Ms. Chase, I must assume my sister did her usual efficient verbal hatchet job on me."

"She had very few kind words to say about you, if that's what you mean."

His eyes glittered darkly. "Yes, that's precisely what I mean. My sister's tongue is as sharp as it is brilliant. You have to admire people like that— even while you're being wary of them. I admit I have a hard time understanding her."

"Sibling rivalry has a way of lasting a lifetime."

"And a very nasty *way* it is."

"However, I've read scientific reports that conclude that drug use alters the user's perception of the people around him."

He regarded me from beneath half-lowered lids with a kind of mercurial alarm. "Well, I see my sister's gone the whole nine yards with you, vomiting up every sick story she can think of."

No wonder Antony Bravanno and Richard Sanborne despised one another. Beneath their different approaches to life, they were very much alike. A deep-seated anger simmered inside them both that could flare up at any time. I had had no previous experience with drugs so I had no way of telling whether, as Jacqueline had said, Antony was a cokehead. But like drugs, ambition had a way of rendering the five senses unreliable.

The edge of the city gave way to the gray metal cage of the Queensboro Bridge. The East River glittered below us; the spires of midtown Manhattan grew insignificant. Framed in the rear window, they had the eye-popping two-dimensionality of a Lichtenstein.

"What else did my sister tell you about me?" he asked with some wariness.

"She said she caught you stealing from your father's businesses. Skimming, I guess you call it."

"Skimming's what we called it before Pop made everything legitimate," he said. "Now there are boards of directors, hosts of accountants, batteries of lawyers, legions of auditors—the same ones who work for AT&T, Ford, and Citibank—to which the officers of each company are held accountable." He smiled. "Skimming isn't the easy proposition it used to be. Even if that's what I had wanted to do. Which, I assure you, it wasn't." He shifted in the plush leather seat. "Pop was training me to take over. Even a warhorse like him was getting tired. He spoke to me more and more often of retiring. The only thing keeping him from taking it easy was that sonuvabitch Sanborne. In a matter of months he would have put everything into my hands. That was the plan, anyway." His sun-bleached eyes bore into mine. "In the face of that, do you think I'd do anything so reckless and stupid as skimming?"

"I can't pretend to know your mind, Mr. Bravanno, but it doesn't seem likely," I admitted.

He nodded. "Damn straight it doesn't." He looked out the window briefly at the huddled squalor of Queens, which had the rough, chaotic characteristics of a third-world bazaar. "Then he was murdered."

"I know. The Russian mafia—"

He stiffened. A dark, flinty look came into his eyes. "The Russian mafia. Is that what she told you?"

"Jacqueline and Sanborne both mentioned it."

"Then they're goddamned liars!" he snarled. Color gathered in his cheeks like Rembrandt shadows as he leaned toward me. "Ms. Chase, let me clue you in. It wasn't the Russians who killed my father, though the people who planned it were clever enough to leave clues around that made it seem as if they had. My dear, sweet sister and her husband had him murdered."

"From everything I've read the Russians are

46

bent on taking over. It makes perfect sense they would—"

"The Russians had nothing of ours before my father was murdered and they have nothing now," Antony said dismissively. "No, I have it on good authority that Sanborne himself carried out the execution. Thought it would make him a made man."

"I've met Sanborne."

"Then I pity you, Ms. Chase, because Richard Sanborne is the devil incarnate. He has no apprehensions, no fear, no scruples, no conscience whatsoever."

"That I can readily believe. But why would Jacqueline take part in scheming to kill her own father?"

"As I said: Richard Sanborne."

"But it seems to me Jacqueline loved your father."

"Maybe, but she's no longer the little girl I grew up with. Since her marriage to Sanborne I wonder what she has become."

"What do you mean?" I demanded.

"We're here," Antony said.

Minutes ago, we had turned into a vast cemetery in Elmont. Now we had stopped at an area laden with floridly carved granite monuments. As

I followed Antony outside I saw that we were at Rocco Bravanno's grave. No one else emerged from the Navigator. A chill wind was blowing. A crow in a tree took off at our arrival, its glossy feathers rainbow-hued like an oil slick in sunlight. A yellow bead of an eye glared at me, then in a flash was gone. The quick of the avian presence brought to life the morbid air of spiritual desolation that informed Van Gogh's *Haystacks.*

Antony took me through a low gate into the family compound. I watched him kneel at his father's grave, make the sign of the cross, and then bend to kiss the cold gray granite. When he rose, his face was as set and graven as the headstone. He lifted an arm, introducing me to a man I had never met and never would meet, at least in this life. There was nothing comical in this introduction; I was reminded again of the black crow, whose gaze had seemed to pierce me to the core.

"My father was old, I can't deny it," Antony said softly, as if speaking to the gathered throng of souls that lay buried beneath his feet. "But he died before his time." He nearly choked on the words. If he was acting, he had missed his calling. "He died like a dog in the gutter. Garbage-stained newspapers were stuffed in his mouth. His body was mutilated, his thumbs cut off." He dropped to his knees, his hands white and clenched, beating at the hard-packed earth. "Sanborne did this to you, Pop; Sanborne you allowed into the family. Ah, God, look how they betrayed you!" He stuffed his knuckles in his mouth and bit down.

It was impossible not to empathize with him. I had had similar feelings about lost opportunities with my own father, who had also died before his time.

Antony rose. Stray clots of dirt clung to his trousers as if the earth in which his father lay was reluctant to let him go. In a somewhat more normal voice, he said to me: "Yesterday you did something very stupid. You fucked me over. You took something that belonged to me. Quite simply, I want it back."

"Jacqueline told me the painting was hers."

"It came from our *father's* vault," he cried, as if I had wounded him. He turned his back to the wind, the better to shield himself from its bite. "It belongs to both of us, yet I have knowledge that Sanborne plans to sell the painting in a private auction."

"Jacqueline will stop him."

"No she won't, because she can't or she doesn't want to. She and Sanborne have had some, ah, difficulties controlling their share of my father's businesses. They need the money."

I turned toward him, acutely aware that he was constantly evaluating me. "Whatever Howard Lenz was or wasn't he didn't deserve to die." I shook my head. "I don't care what you say, I want no part of your blood feud."

"It's too late," he said brusquely. "You're already a part of it."

"Perhaps, inadvertently, I was. No good deed goes unpunished. But I won't do anything to help you."

"I can see you're a strong-willed woman," he said. "But before you make your decision final you ought to be aware that there was nothing inadvertent about your involvement." Taking a step toward me, he held up a hand. "Have you asked yourself how Carmine and Leon knew you had the painting?"

"I suppose they—" I stopped. "They could have followed me from the scene of the accident."

"Do you think they did? Did you ever see them before they burst into your apartment?"

"No," I said, thoughtfully.

"And how is it, do you think, they showed up just after you made your discovery of the Raphael? Should we assume it was merely a coincidence?" He took my elbow in a repugnantly familiar fashion. "Ms. Chase, you said before that you thought I was lying to you. What if I could not only demonstrate my good faith, but at the same time prove that in fact it's my sister who is lying to you."

"I doubt you can do that."

"Indulge me this one time. Believe me, I have your best interest in mind."

While it was clear to me that Antony had in mind no one's best interest but his own, I knew he was giving me no other choice but to assent.

He began to lead me back to the Navigator. "This is something you need to see for yourself."

When we arrived at my loft, Antony asked me to lead him to my study. Once there, he said, "I want you to look in the upper right-hand corner."

I peered up to where the ceiling met the walls. A thick fluted plaster molding ran around the entire room.

"Can't find it? It's in the molding." He watched me with calm eyes as I dragged a chair over and stood on it. Reaching up, I could feel the glass of the lens of the remote-controlled miniature video camera. My face drained of color. There was a roaring in my ears and I felt my pulse hammering in my chest.

"Tiny, isn't it? Nowadays, it's all done with fiber optics," he said as I looked down at him. "That's how they knew when to show up. They saw everything you were doing."

"How long has it been there?"

He shrugged. "That I couldn't say. I just hope they didn't let Leon get a peek at you."

Even without him saying that I felt invaded, humiliated, violated. What was the punishment for electronic rape? I wondered. "How do I know you didn't plant this?"

"If I had I wouldn't need you to get the painting back." He was right; Jacqueline had lied to me, used me. Now I remembered the expression on Lenz's face when he had seen me just before he had been killed. He'd been looking for me at the museum; from the first, he had been given instructions to bring the painting to me. "And, if you're wondering," Antony went on, "I found out about the camera too late to act except in the way I have."

I got off my perch.

"I'll remove it for you," he said. "It won't take but a minute."

"I don't need you for that," I told him as I took up one of my scraping implements. Jumping back onto the chair, I got a measure of satisfaction by jabbing the point through the lens.

But it wasn't enough, not nearly, and so I looked into that Picasso face. I might have felt better in my heart if I had hesitated even a second, but I didn't. "You said you want to get the painting back. If you do, what will you do with it?"

"I sure as hell won't auction it off like that sonuvabitch Sanborne will."

"I want it donated to the Empire Museum. You can make it in your father's name."

"Done and done," he said without hesitation.

Even though I didn't believe him, I heard myself say: "What is it you want me to do?"

The Bravanno compound appeared larger than life when I arrived the next morning. As I drove my car through the gates, I saw a couple of guards eyeing me. The house still seemed grand, but now it appeared shrouded in darker hues, as if the tainted insides had begun to leach out like poison.

It was Carmine who met me in the entryway. "Good morning, Ms. Chase. This is a surprise," he said, neither smiling nor frowning, "Mr. Sanborne is in the city on business."

"I can wait," I said. "In the meantime, I want to see Jacqueline."

"Ah, Miss Jacqueline is upstairs," he said, referring to her as if she were an eight-year-old without a will of her own. "Unfortunately, she's feeling under the weather. Is there something I can do for you?"

"You can tell her I'm here," I said as I began to walk around him.

"I'm afraid I can't do that." He moved to block me. "I have my orders."

"Whose orders?" I said, moving the other way. "Sanborne's?"

He blocked my way again. "It's no concern of yours."

I ignored him. "Tell me, Carmine, was it you who installed the remote video camera in my loft?"

"I don't know what you're talking about," he said, sphinxlike.

"I'll just bet you don't," I said as I tromped on his instep with my high heel. A little squeal came out of his mouth and I ducked under his wildly swinging arm, gained the stairs and bolted up them.

"You bitch," he growled, losing his sangfroid. "I know you like to work in your skimpy bra and panties. Leon got off on that." He had a murderous look in his eyes as he came after me. I knew how much it must have hurt him every time he put weight on his bruised foot, and was glad of it.

There was music coming from the bedroom at the left end of the upper floor, *Afternoon of a Faun*, and I followed it as if I was Debussy's magical animal. Carmine was close behind me as I ran down the thickly-carpeted hallway, and as I reached the open doorway, he lunged, grabbed my left arm, and began to swing me around. The pastoral melody swirled incongruously around us as I slammed the back of his encircling hand against the doorjamb. He twisted my arm. I felt a pain run up my forearm and then Jacqueline was saying: "Let her go, Carmine."

Standing there in a plush pink bathrobe she looked like an elegant flamingo.

"But Mr. Sanborne left instructions—"

"I said, let her go," she commanded in a voice so stark Carmine took his hand off me. "Now get back downstairs."

Carmine glared at me. With a quick glance at Jacqueline, he turned on his heel and clomped away.

She smiled. "Tess, I'm so happy to see you."

"That won't last," I said as I dug into the pocket of my overcoat. I threw the damaged video camera onto the bed. It lay there, gravid with incrimination, against the pale froth of the satin duvet cover.

She looked at it in horror. "Oh, hell, how did you find it?" At least she had the decency not to lie to me about it as Carmine had.

"Antony brought it to my attention," I said coldly.

"That sonuvabitch. I was getting up the courage to tell you myself. See, I did my research; I knew Howard Lenz's reputation. I needed someone to make sure Lenz didn't suddenly decide to screw Richard over."

"And you think that gave you the right to spy on me—to invade my privacy?"

"I don't trust anyone. But that was before I met you. Before . . . ." She took my hand. "Tess, I can't tell you how sorry I am." I tried to snatch it away, but she gasped: "My God, you're bleeding."

I looked down, saw the blood crawling down the back of my left hand where Carmine had twisted it against the doorjamb. Jacqueline was already herding me into a huge, luxurious bath-room caparisoned with orchids of all sizes and descriptions. Rather truculently, I agreed to sit on the upholstered stool in front of her vanity while she went to work cleaning the wound first with soap and water, then an anti-bacterial spray.

"It's deep, but otherwise not so bad," she said. She had an exceptionally gentle touch.

"Jacqueline, you lied to me about something else."

She had been kneeling in front of me, wrap-ping the bandage. Now she sat back on her haunches and looked at me. "What do you mean?"

"I know about how you and your husband schemed to get rid of your father."

Her face drained of color. For a moment she seemed at a loss for words. Then, the blood rushed back into her face and she said: "That can't be *all* you know. Tell me the rest of it."

"But you already—"

"Tell me!" she cried with such genuine anguish that I complied. I told her how Antony had taken me to the cemetery in Elmont, and what he had told me there, about how she had conspired with Sanborne to murder Rocco and make it look like the Russian mafia had committed the crime.

To this damning testimony she said not a word, but abruptly rose and went to the casement window. The screeching sound her nails made when she raked them down the tile wall made me shudder. I discovered, to my shock, that the anger I had felt only a moment ago was being leached away simply by my proximity to her. I found myself frightened by the intensity of my feelings. I felt stripped naked in front of her, harrowed to my soul. It was easy—even highly pleasurable—for me to feel this way about a painting; to be so vulnerable to another human being filled me with alarm. But, astonishingly, that was not all I was feeling. It was the dreadful elation one experiences in a careening car that has gone out of control.

"I'm never going to be free from their lies and scheming," she whispered. She turned back to me. "These men who surround me, who keep me pinned in place, are ruled by their ambition. It doesn't matter a damn who they hurt in the process." She knelt again in front of me, gathered my hands gently in hers. "Tess, I swear on the soul of my mother I had nothing to do with my father's death. I would rather put a knife in my heart than harm him. My God, you have only to see what's happened to me since his death to know I'm telling the truth."

I peered deep into her eyes and believed her. The one thing she and Antony had in common was their undeniable love for Rocco. So Antony was only half-right. Sanborne had pulled the trigger but Jacqueline had known nothing about it.

"Jacqueline, you understand that it's Sanborne who has gained the most by your father's death."

Apparently, she didn't trust herself to speak; nevertheless, the look in her eyes showed me that she had harbored doubts about his Russian mafia story. That hadn't meant she hadn't made herself believe it. I could understand that, because it was simply easier to accept betrayal on that scale by people she did not know.

"How I hate Richard," she said when she had sorted through all her conflicting emotions.

"You're not alone," I said.

She began to weep. "What am I to do?"

Disengaging myself from her, I went to the window where I could at least reassure myself that there was a world larger than this suite of rooms. Staring out into the flood-lit night, I said: "You know a lot of inside information—the kind the feds would jump all over. I have no doubt that in exchange for your testimony they could extract you, hide you, even change your identity after you were through testifying."

She came up behind me, grabbed me and, whirled me around. "Is that what you think I should do? Bring down everything my father worked for?" she cried.

"I think it may be time to bring it down."

She slapped me across the face, and was going to do it again when I grabbed her wrist.

"Yes, yes, I'll become a whore to the feds," she hissed. "I'll rat out my brother and then let them throw me into some dark corner. My God, Tess, don't you see what you're asking me to do?"

"You're already in a very dark corner," I said.

"But I'm not a rat. I couldn't live with the shame if I betrayed my father and my brother." I felt her twisting her wrist to get free. "I won't be the next Sammy the Bull, oh, God, don't ask that of me."

"I only want to keep you from harm."

"Then save me, Tess. Save me."

Before I knew what I was doing, my lips came down over hers, my mouth opened and our tongues twined. I felt as well as heard her words, the vibrations rippling down by entire body. I was unable to resist her in the same way I was unable to resist the first Monet I had bought. I had seen it at an auction in Paris and my knees had gone weak. I knew then that I would buy it no matter the cost. Money was no object and neither was reason. It had possessed me, just as Jacqueline possessed me now.

With a soft moan, I broke away from her and, without an instant even to say goodbye, fled back through her bedroom and out the door. There was a guard at the foot of the stairs, and though he had not yet seen me, I knew I could not face him. Glancing about, I chanced to see another, narrower back staircase, and I hastened down this before Jacqueline could collect herself sufficiently to come after me.

Downstairs, I found myself in the mudroom, which I hurried through. I pushed open the back door, went left to go around the house to my car. Just shy of the corner, my knees failed me and I paused, leaning back against the cedar boards as the shivers went through me. I tried unsuccessfully to calm the fierce pounding of my heart.

That was when I heard his voice.

At first, I assumed Carmine was speaking to one of the other guards, but when there was no reply and he continued speaking I knew he must be using a cellular phone.

"That's right," he was saying, "I made it hard for her just like you said . . . I don't know, they've been up in Jacqueline's bedroom for close to thirty minutes . . ." He guffawed; it was an unexpectedly coarse noise, like a fart. "Fuckin' Leon was drooling after the art broad so bad I had to put him on perimeter duty. . . ." He lowered his voice but, apparently, he had come closer to where I was standing because I could hear with startling clarity how convincingly he had switched from the artful diction he used when speaking to me. "Listen, after the old man bought it you promised me a family of my own. So far, whatta I got? *Ugatz*, that's what . . . Whaddya mean, be patient. That's what the old man useta tell me and look how that's turned out . . . I know you told me you gotta be cautious before you move against Sanborne, but meanwhile I'm stuck here with my thumb up my ass just so I won't fuckin' blow the sonuvabitch away every time he opens his pretentious yap. And, I gotta be honest now and no disrespect intended, but the thought, y'know, here and there crosses my mind maybe you're all talk and no action . . . Right, I gotcha, okay,

I'd never talk to the old man that way, but, y'know, Ant'ny, you're not the old man—at least, not yet . . . Really? Well, I mean to say a lotta guys of my acquaintance are lookin' your way to see if you got the balls to step into the old man's shoes, so don't bite my fuckin' head off, because I'm your eyes and ears around here, y'know . . . Yeah, right. But, Christ almighty, I tell ya, I'm just fuckin' fed up with this spy shit. I'm from the old school—badda-bing, badda-bam, badda-boom. That's how we took care of things in the old days . . . Sure, sure, I know it's not the old fuckin' days no more, I'm just saying . . . Right, okay . . . So maybe this art broad will do the trick, like you say, and we can wipe the slate clean. . . . " He chuckled deep in his throat. "I'll say this for her, she sure got a pair on her."

My face was tight and burning. I barely dared to breathe. If Carmine should come around the corner. . . . But he didn't. He finished his conversation with Antony Bravanno and went back to the front of the house the way he had come.

I gave myself over to the small pleasure of inhaling the fresh air. Leaning my head back against the side of the house, I stared up at the sky where an infinite blue had fused itself behind the lush branches of the trees. Once, in Italy after a car accident, I sat staring out a windshield shattered to a Whistler latticework, the beauty of the world beyond transformed by trauma. Now shocking events had conspired to recreate this vision. An eerie, almost palpable stillness had stolen across the property that somehow gave great weight to each following thought and movement. No wonder Antony had it on good authority that Sanborne had murdered Rocco; Carmine had told him. Now that I knew Carmine was secretly working for Antony I discovered I had no intention of heading for my car. Instead, I turned around and went back upstairs.

Jacqueline sat at the end of the bed, clad only in panties, her head in her hands. She looked up at my approach.

"Did you know I'd come back?" I asked her.

She walked over to me and, grabbing the back of my head, kissed me hard. I felt her breasts against mine, felt her pelvis grind into me, felt my blood boiling in my veins, my thighs turning to jelly. I felt as if I had two hearts, one beating in my chest, the other throbbing between my thighs. I pushed against her and she backed up. I kept pushing while I kissed her until the bed came up behind her and we both dissolved onto it.

"I want to be with you forever." She moaned into my mouth, and kept on moaning as I opened her legs with my thigh.

Through the early stages, we looked into each other's eyes, something I had never done with any other lover. We were totally and exquisitely naked watching each other's emotions chase one another across our faces. Then the roughened outer layers were one by one stripped away like the leaves of an artichoke, revealing the inner petals: increasingly paler, more delicate, more delicious, until together we ravished the impossibly tender hearts.

What she liked to do afterward, I quickly learned, was lick the salty sweat off me, and that set me off all over again.

Darkness, crawling across the hardwood floor, lapped at where we lay, entwined in the vinelike bedcovers. I could hear her steady, even breathing and I longed for the unconsciousness that had taken her up in its arms, but I was too preoccupied. In my mind's eye I saw the darkness of my loft. I had always been grateful for the candles' glow—as if their illumination signaled a reawakening of the golden ages of history. But it seemed to me now that the comfort I had gained in the company of this host of great art had something of the nature of the worldly possessions amassed by the Egyptian pharaohs on their final journey downward into the earth. I had been for some time, it seemed, buried with my art in my own self-made tomb, adoring them—oh, so safely!—instead of grappling with the fearful joy, the fearsome anguish that ensued from intimate human contact.

After my mother deserted him, my father made no attempt to re-marry or even to court another woman. No doubt being hurt once in just that way had been enough for him. Lying against Jacqueline's softly breathing body I asked a question that kept dumb sleep on a distant shore: Was I then so much like him? It seemed to me that my father paid a terrible price for falling in love that had nothing whatsoever to do with my mother. In the face of her treachery he could not continue, at least not along that particular path.

In the delicious cool dimness of the bedroom Jacqueline shared with Richard Sanborne, I could smell our musk combining in a way that set my pulse to pounding. I could not get enough of her, and I grew afraid. But then I saw again in my mind's eye my candle-bright loft, and I was struck by the depth of the shadows that had gathered in the corners without my notice. If I allowed myself this love, I would in some fashion alter my connection to my paintings, but at the same time, I knew, the darkness growing there would be obliged to melt away in the furnace of that unique heat.

I lay for a time, my mind processing these thoughts and images at lightning speed yet, curiously, the minutes passed with unnatural graduation. When, at length, Jacqueline stirred, I told her about the conversation between Carmine and her brother.

"That's good," she said, propping herself up on one elbow.

"How can it be good?"

"Because it's knowledge, and knowledge is power." I could see her silhouette limned in the hard bluish glow of the security lights that illuminated the compound. "I suspected Antony must have a spy close to Richard, I just didn't know who. Now I do."

"There's more," I said. "Antony sent me back here for a specific purpose. He wants me to convince you and Sanborne that I have a buyer for the Raphael—a client whose offer is so high Sanborne's greed would outweigh any suspicions he might harbor."

I saw Jackie's head turn. "How high?"

"Fifty-five million."

"Madonna!" She threw her head back and laughed.

"What's funny about that?" I asked.

She slithered across the bed to wrap herself around me. She was still hot from our lovemaking. "Two days ago my knees would have gone weak at the thought of getting so much money, and God forgive me, I would have used you just like my brother is trying to use you to get it." She kissed me. "Now I don't give a damn." She ran her fingers through my hair. "I don't give a damn about anything but you." Her eyes searched mine. "Tess, I love you so much. I swear I'll never hurt you again. Do you believe me, at least a little bit?"

"I want to believe you," I said.

I saw a tear well up at the corner of her eye and she kissed me. "When I was little," she said, "my mother took me every week to see my grandmother. At first, I was a brat. I would rather have been out playing than be cooped up in a huge, dark room that smelled of powdered flesh and mothballs. But gradually I came to like it there, and to look forward to the visits. This was due entirely to my grandmother. She had been an invalid for some time and, as compensation I suppose, had developed a beguiling personality. I liked her most because she didn't treat me the way the other adults did. She spoke to me as a compatriot if not an equal—we both knew I had too much to learn! She taught me lessons and told me secrets. 'Resist with all your soul the overtures of others who tell you how you must live,' she said to me. 'Above all, beware of all men, because no matter if they love you or not, they will try to take that life from you so you can become a part of theirs.'

"Strangely, my mother disliked her own mother; she believed her wicked, and only visited her out of a heightened sense of filial duty. Each week, after our visit, she would take me straight to church as if she had to cleanse me. As she thrust me into the confessional she would hiss: 'Tell the father what the old woman whispered in your ear.' Frightened, I would do as she said, and afterward the father always said: 'Your penance is to recite ten Hail Marys and ten Our Fathers,' just as if I had sinned." Her gaze glided over my face. "I wonder if I say ten Hail Marys and ten Our Fathers now whether God will forgive me for spying on you."

Her eyes closed and she seemed to melt as I licked her ear. "If I forgive you, He must forgive you as well."

"My grandmother was very wise," she said, putting her head into the crook of my neck.

I pushed her a little away from me. "We should just leave now while we can, before everything escalates out of control."

She shook her head. "It's too late for that. Richard will send people after us, and I have no illusions about us evading them permanently." She gave me a melancholy smile as she squeezed my hand. "Besides, running, hiding, that's no life for either of us."

"Then we'll go to Antony."

"My brother despises me."

"But we'll have the Raphael. We'll give it to him in exchange for your freedom."

The smile underwent a subtle transformation from mere melancholy to outright sadness. "How little you know my brother. Antony is a traditionalist in all things. He knows nothing about my private predilections and thank God for that! If he even had a hint about us he'd kill you himself and lock me away."

"He can't have that much power." But even as I said it the force of my indignation dissipated in the cauldron of her forbidding expression.

"Tell me the details of Antony's plan," she said.

"He has given me a hundred thousand dollars to use as this fictitious client's show of good faith. Sanborne will take it; we both know he's greedy

70

as sin. I'm to set the meet for tomorrow at three A.M. at the Bethesda fountain in Central Park. Antony assures me Sanborne will want the balance of the fifty-five million deposited in the Bahamanian bank he uses. After I have the Raphael and have authenticated it, I'm to make a call to initiate the electronic transfer. Apparently, when you're moving this much money around, this kind of bank never sleeps. Sanborne will call his bank for verification, except Antony will have one of his own people take the call, and someone will put a bullet through the back of Sanborne's head. Now we know it will be Carmine, because there's no doubt Carmine will be with Sanborne at the meet."

"What did my brother promise you for your role in this?" she asked.

"He said he would let me donate the Raphael to the museum."

"You know there's no chance of that ever happening."

"Of course. Which is why you're going to convince Sanborne not to take the deal."

Curious. This exchange had only quickened her interest. "The real question is how would we take care of Carmine?" she mused. "It's obvious he can't be trusted now or ever."

I considered a moment, and a clever, reckless thought came into my head. "All right, spinning out this little fairy tale to the bitter end, *if* this were going to happen—which it is not—I would plant a seed of doubt in Carmine's mind. It's clear he doesn't entirely trust your brother, he just needs his power to get what he thinks he deserves. I would whisper to him that Antony has no intention of giving him his own family."

"My brother takes care of Richard, and Carmine and Antony are immediately at each other's throats. It's absolutely perfect." Her eyes glittered in the semi-darkness. "Let's do it."

"What?" My stomach turned to ice. "Are you out of your mind?" But I knew she wasn't; knew, further, deep down where I did not care to look very often, this was how she would respond. "That was just a fantasy, a game," I protested. "I am not going to be a party to anyone's death, not even people as evil as these men." But I wondered who was kidding whom.

She gripped my shoulders. "Come on, Tess. Think! It's my only way out of here." She gave me a look that could melt ice. "Even if Richard dies, Antony will still be around. We'll never be able to see each other again. Is that what you want?"

"No, it isn't. But—"

"But nothing. This kind of opportunity happens once in a lifetime—and only then if you're very lucky." Her voice was infused with the ardor that made sex with her so compelling. "Luck's with us, Tess. We have only to reach out and snatch it up."

It was odd. At that moment, I could imagine her as a little girl, advancing gravely to her grandmother's bedside, where she knelt while the old woman whispered forcefully in her ear. I could feel a cloak of the old woman's design closing over us. I knew I was in over my head, but what could I do; I was in the grip of a fever I was ill-equipped to handle. My father had trained me for every eventuality save the quixotic eruption of my own intimate emotions. The thought of abandoning Jacqueline to what amounted to solitary confinement was intolerable. Something had to be done and, toward that end she was correct, we had been given an enormous gift. In a sense, the ambition that drove these men—Sanborne, Antony, and Carmine—was nothing more than naked greed; and by a twist of fate their ambition could be turned against them—and to our everlasting advantage. Why not take what fate was offering us? I asked myself. It would, in fact, be stupid not to.

"All right," I said with the slow, rather anguished thud one feels when agreeing to a major medical operation. It was the right course of action—the only course of action under the circumstances—but damn these men to hell if the taste of blood wasn't already in my mouth.

L et me see it. All of it."

Sanborne had cut me off in mid-sentence. Of course. Antony had been right on the mark. What he cared most about was the money. I took the bills out of the worn leather satchel Antony had provided, and stacked them up for him.

"No, no," he said with some irritation. "Spread them out. Didn't I say I wanted to see it all?" When the money covered the coffee table, he snapped his fingers. Carmine appeared as if out of nowhere. "Count it," Sanborne said as Jacqueline poured Sambuca into his coffee cup.

"A hundred thou, even," Carmine said as he stood up. "Kosher as Passover."

With a languid motion that belied the avaricious look in his eyes, Sanborne took the coffee from Jacqueline. For a time, he sat sipping, his heavy, loaded gaze on the money.

"All right," he said at last. "Let's hear the rest of it."

I told him about the deal as Antony had laid it out for me.

"So who is this guy, your client?" Sanborne said when I was through giving him the particulars.

"He's a European financier. That's all I can tell you."

He put his cup down. "Then it's no dice."

But his eyes never left the money and I knew he was hooked. "Mr. Sanborne, in my business discretion is everything. If I made a habit of revealing clients' identities when it is their express wish to remain anonymous I very quickly would have no clients."

"Make an exception this one time. For me."

"I'm sorry."

"I'll pay you handsomely for the information."

I began to gather up the bills. "It's impossible."

"Wait." Now he looked at me. "You have integrity. That's an admirable trait." He tapped his forefinger on the stack of money. "Forty-five million, you said. Do you think he'll go higher?"

I pretended to consider this a moment. "Fifty-five, but I know positively that is his limit."

Sanborne smiled up at me and said with the auctioneer's facile enthusiasm, "Sold American."

I waited a nervous hour after Carmine dropped me off at the loft before venturing out. Even then, I made sure no one was around, and took a circuitous route west. Bob Hodges opened the door to his and Nina's Greenwich Village brownstone when I knocked.

"Hey," he smiled and gave me a big hug. "Now this is a surprise."

"Bob, I'm in trouble," I said as he took my coat and led me through the foyer.

"I'll get Nina," he replied without another word.

I threw myself down on the comfortable oversized sofa in the living room, only to jump up again as soon as Bob came back with his wife. Nina Hodges was the assistant chief federal prosecutor for the Southern District. As such, she was hip-deep in the big time crime that was endemic to New York. This tall dark-haired woman with a sleek figure and a frighteningly keen mind embraced me, told me how good I looked, and then said, "What kind of trouble are you in, Tess?"

So I told them everything I had learned about the internal feud between the Bravannos. I did not leave out my feelings for Jacqueline, since they were central to my dilemma.

Bob, ever the emotional one, said, "Jesus Christ."

"Bob, be a love and get us all some coffee, would you?" Nina said in her kindest voice. Then she came and sat next to me on the sofa, her legs tucked up under her. Because of this habit, Bob liked to call her his cat. Cute. But I knew from the cases she tried that this was one cat with very sharp claws.

"Bring Jacqueline Bravanno to me," she said. "In exchange for her testimony we will protect her, give her a new life. You know the drill."

"I do, but in this case it's not an option." I could feel the sadness welling up inside me. "I've tried to convince her, but she's adamant in refusing to testify against her family."

"Then I advise you to get out as expeditiously as possible," Nina said in a measured tone. "In fact, it's good you're here. Don't go back. Stay for a while—as long as you want, actually. You know we have plenty of room."

"I can't tell you how tempting that sounds." I shook my head. "But the way I feel about her . . . I can't simply abandon her to her fate. It would be inhuman."

She took my hands in hers. "Look, Tess, I've known you for a long time. You have this special quality when you choose to express it that so beautifully combines love and compassion. You're far more courageous than most people. No one could appreciate that more than I do, but, my God, you're in a highly volatile and dangerous situation."

"I know. Strangely enough I can live with that." I met her steady gaze with my own. "It's the guilt that would tear me apart if I turned tail and ran out on her."

"Are you sure she's worth it?"

Bob returned with a tray laden with a coffeepot, cups, and a box of Mallomars. He set it down between us and poured. The rich aroma swirled in a heady bouquet, but neither of us moved.

"What's going on?" he said, looking from me to his wife and back again.

"If you've become involved to that extent," Nina said to me in that same measured tone, "I honestly don't know whether I can help you."

"Nina. For God's sake, this is Tess."

I lifted a hand. "It's all right, Bob." To Nina, I said: "I understand. I know you'll help me if you can."

She seemed deathly calm, resigned even. "It can't end well, you know. It never does."

"I'm her only hope. Without me she'll never get out."

"It's you I'm worried about."

"I'll be fine," I said with as much bravado as I could muster.

"I have to ask you again, Tess: is she worth it?"

"She's chained and bound, not only by tradition but by all the men in her life. She's desperate to break free of their control but you know what these men are like—you can't simply walk away from them." I looked into Nina's eyes. "To some extent, we've all been there, we've all felt the kinds of power men have to bind us to them."

This curiously quiet exchange was, underneath, an altogether ferocious test of wills, as if Nina needed to plumb the depth of my resolve. She reached over for her coffee, apparently thought better of it, and rose. "Excuse me a moment."

There was an uncomfortable silence after she left, punctuated by the brass ship's clock on the mantle. It chimed the watch change, rather than the hour, but by any measure time was still passing. Bob and I ate Mallomars while I looked at the Persian carpet and he tapped his feet mindlessly. We were good friends, too close to make small talk when each minute seemed unnaturally momentous.

When Nina returned there was a curious look on her face. "There may be a way," she said as she sat again beside me. "I made some calls, pulled in some favors and . . . Look, Tess, I have no business telling you this—it's strictly against regulations, but if you're determined to go back to that snake pit I can't in all good conscience let you do it naked." She drew a breath. "The Bravannos have been the subject of a long-running investigation."

"I haven't heard anything about that," Bob said.

"No one has, and no one will until it's all over," Nina replied tensely. "That's because it's been all undercover. Which is why I'm going way out on a limb by mentioning it even this once." She licked her lips. "There's an agent in place—a federal agent who specializes in such things. He's managed to work his way up the family hierarchy. Stay close to him, Tess, when the shit hits the fan and you'll be okay."

"What's his name?" I asked.

"It's this man Carmine you spoke of. He's one of ours."

B ethesda fountain at a quarter to three in the morning was not a spot I would voluntarily choose to go. Neither would most other people, which was one of the reasons Antony had targeted it. The other was that although it was a wide open plaza in the European fashion, which would appeal to Sanborne's acute attention to security, it was overlooked by wide stairs guarded by stone parapets. The low foliage just beyond would serve to effectively conceal any observer who wanted to remain hidden.

It was raining just enough to be uncomfortable. The slicked-down roadways shimmered in the lavender-white sodium lights. A freakish mist had risen through the trees, severing the park from the comforting solidity of the surrounding skyscrapers. Colors were drawn off like juices from an overdone roast, leaving a void between the stark black ironwork and the goblinlike whiteness of the plane trees and the cement. Intermittent traffic hissed by no closer than the distant rumble of thunder.

I stood, as instructed, with my back to the stairs. I could see my short, sharp exhalations exploding in little bursts of bleached vapor, and I spent the remaining time until three in an attempt to regulate my breathing. The worst thing I could do now was hyperventilate and fill my body with carbon dioxide. No, the worst thing I could do was turn and run.

I heard the scrape of shoe soles against concrete and, turning my head, I could see Sanborne and Carmine advancing toward me from the other side of the fountain. Then my heart skipped a beat. Jacqueline was with them, just as we had planned. With the knowledge Nina had given me my view of Carmine had been drastically altered. All of a sudden, he had become the lifeline for me and Jacqueline, the bastion of law and order in a bleak landscape of treachery and crime.

"You ready to make the call?" Sanborne smiled at me without actually seeing me; he was too busy trying to look at everything at once. I showed him my cell phone and he pointed at the package beneath Jackie's arm. "There's the Raphael." I noticed Carmine's big, square hands hanging loosely at his side.

I went over to where they stood. "I need to see the Raphael to authenticate it."

"Be my guest," Sanborne said, "but there won't be any surprises."

"I hope not." I slipped the package out of Jacqueline's grasp without managing to meet her gaze and stepped back. I took a good, hard look at the Raphael while Carmine took out a cell phone.

"I'm satisfied," I said, re-wrapping the precious painting. I made the call, keeping my voice up so Sanborne could clearly hear me order the transfer of funds.

Sanborne snapped his fingers, Carmine handed him his cell phone, and, in one fluid motion, withdrew his Glock. By the long-nosed silhouette I knew it was silenced. Quickly but calmly he pressed the muzzle against the base of Sanborne's skull and fired two shots. Sanborne, his eyes open wide in shock, pitched forward onto his face. He was dead so fast he didn't even have time to twitch.

As if that had been a sign, Antony and that Goliath Louie came loping down the stairs. Antony, his eyes shining, made a great whooping noise. He was grinning from ear to ear as Carmine shot him squarely between the eyes. Antony's legs turned to spaghetti and he danced an impromptu spastic jig. Louie had his gun out before his boss collapsed onto the paving, but Carmine was ready for him, and took him down as well with two perfectly placed shots.

"Always aim for the head," he said as he surveyed the carnage. Then he looked at both of us.

"You gals okay? Not gonna toss your cookies or nothing, are ya?"

Jacqueline shook her head mutely. Her eyes were glued over as if she were in shock.

"Don't worry," I said to her. "Carmine is a fed."

His eyes narrowed, "Where'd you hear that?"

"Deep Throat."

He laughed and snapped his fingers at me. "Okie dokie, lady, give me the Raphael."

With a profound sense of relief, I handed over the painting. I was thinking how oddly tainted it had become, how the evil of its recent history would now be off my hands when he turned the Glock on me. "Now get over by your little pal."

My stomach turned to water. "What the hell is going on? You're supposed to—"

He aimed the Glock at a point between my eyes. "Just do as I say!" he barked.

I went over and took Jacqueline's hand. "I don't get it," I said. "What do you think you're doing?"

"Just doin' what comes naturally." He grinned at me. "You think I wanna go back to making a lousy thirty g's a year when I can make that in ten minutes staying here? Watta you, nuts? No, thank you very much, I'm in a perfect fuckin' position now. I've taken care of all my rivals; I can say with a great deal of justification that they whacked each other. Why not? They woulda done it in a heart-beat. Now I'm king of the hill. The Bravanno family is mine to run."

"Don't be a fool," I said. "Your people will never let you get away with it."

"Listen, lady, the feds don't know squat. They haven't a clue half the stuff I've been up to. You think they even suspect I whacked Rocco? No way, baby. No one knew, not Sanborne, not Antony, no one. They all believed what I told 'em." He winked at me. "See, I know how to feed the feds, give them what they want up to a point and they don't know the diff. Not unless you and the lovely Miss Jacqueline here tell them." The Glock twitched in his hand. "Which you won't because in two seconds you're both gonna be dead."

"MARTY, GIVE IT UP," a voice hollered through a portable loud-speaker. The three of us looked up to see armed personnel. They were clad in distinctive dark-blue slickers with large white "FBI" imprinted on them, massing along the parapet.

"IT'S ALL OVER, MARTY," the voice continued. "PUT DOWN YOUR WEAPON AND

SURRENDER. YOU HAVE NO OTHER CHOICE."

Carmine turned to me, that murderous look in his eye. "Fuck! You did this to me, you whore-bitch! Who told you about me? Who did you spill your guts to?"

I didn't think he would shoot, not with all the agents taking aim at him, but I was wrong. Just before he pulled the trigger, Jacqueline moved. She knew him far better than I did. She couldn't move far because our fingers were still twined, but it was enough. I didn't even have time to react. I was screaming my warning when the bullet smashed through the side of her skull and into my left shoulder. She fell back against me, alabaster arms gently spread like the Madonna's in the *Pietà*, her blood all over me, but I had the Tomcat out and was squeezing off a shot that spun Carmine around. He fired blindly into the air and a hail of gunfire blew him away from us as if he were a dry leaf in the wind.

I was down on my knees, sick and numb with shock, cradling Jacqueline's head in my lap, sticky with blood, when I saw Nina running toward me. She was cloaked in one of those FBI slickers and she kept waving her arms to keep the others back. They had enough to do, anyway, checking the other bodies.

"Tess." She knelt down beside me.

"I promised I'd protect her," I said through the tears streaming down my cheeks. "I could have saved her, but I didn't shoot him fast enough."

"Don't do this," she said. "How could you know? The sonuvabitch was supposed to be on our side, and bless you, you shot him before he could hit any of our men." Then she saw the blood pumping slowly out of my shoulder, and she shouted for the EMS paramedics before turning back to me. "Tess, are you all right?"

"I don't know." I gathered Jacqueline's lifeless body to me and rocked her a little. "Ask me next month or next year. But not now."

I felt Nina's warmth as she held me, as she said to me, "Don't worry. I'll take care of you. Everything's going to be okay."

I heard her without really believing what she said. I had already begun reciting ten Hail Marys and ten Our Fathers, but at that moment, with Jacqueline lying heavy against me, forgiveness seemed part of a world that would never again be within my reach.